# MAIL ORDER BRIDE: CATHERINE

## THE COURAGEOUS ORPHAN BRIDES

### CASSIE MALONE

LIVE LIFE FULLY MEDIA

ISBN: 978-1-63536-021-9

# 1

St. Louis, Missouri, early June 1881...

C atherine Lamott sat in the park next to the river and watched the riverboats roll by. Today was her nineteenth birthday, but it was unlike any previous year where she'd celebrated the event of her birth with a party, presents, and her family gathered around her. This year, she was alone.

Completely, utterly alone.

Her father had come home sick three months earlier with a mysterious illness, and then her mother and her little sister had gotten sick. Catherine had been away at school on the East Coast. When she'd finally been summoned home, it had been too late to say her final farewells to her family and she arrived instead to make funeral arrangements for them.

She'd refused to return to school although it was her last year, with only two months left until graduation. She'd stayed in St. Louis to try to understand what had happened. Her father had taken it into his head to become a great adventurer and had gone on an expedition to some of the northern territories. Unfortunately, he'd brought home an illness that had not only taken the lives of his wife and young daughter, but more than half of the household staff had fallen ill and died.

The local authorities, fearful that the illness might spread, had demanded the house and all of its possessions be burned to the ground. She had returned home with her luggage containing her clothing and a few books and personal affects, but everything else had been reduced to a blackened, charred mess by the time she had arrived on the train.

To make matters even worse, she'd been the only one besides a few remaining staff members to attend the funeral. Everyone else had stayed away lest they catch whatever had taken the lives of Charles Lamott and his lovely wife and daughter. After the funeral, she'd bid a tearful farewell to the remaining staff, unable to keep them employed as there was no house to maintain.

Since arriving in St. Louis, she had been living either out of a hotel room, or out of the rented boarding house room she was currently residing in to save her limited funds. Her father's money hadn't been burned – safely tucked away inside a local bank, and initially she'd thought she had more than enough to start a new life. Those thoughts were fleeting and within a week, she knew there were going to be some problems.

She had become an outcast amongst the people who had known her since birth. None of her father's closest friends would meet with her. News of her father's demise had spread across the region, and even her father's business associates, ones he had made very wealthy, had started withdrawing their funds and their support.

The banks had called in the loans her father owed, and now, three weeks later, she wasn't destitute, but closer than she liked to admit. She had six hundred dollars, a rented room for the rest of the month, and no prospects for her future.

Her long standing fiancé, who had promised he was waiting for her to return from school so they could marry, had disappeared when her father's fortune started to dwindle. Apparently, he was looking for a society princess, and she no longer qualified.

She sighed and looked down at the pastry she'd purchased from a street vendor. At one point in time, she'd thought her life was perfect. Now, she wasn't even sure she had a life to call her own. She tried to find the upside to everything that had happened, but even though the sun was shining and a clear blue sky stood overhead, all she saw were storm clouds in her future.

"Happy birthday to me," she whispered aloud. She sniffed back the tears, refusing to feel sorry for herself a moment longer. She ate the pastry, and then strolled along the river front until the sun began to go down. She returned to her small room in the boarding house, and fell asleep in a chair, sitting next to the open window. The moon was her companion in those moments and as she drifted off to sleep, she wondered what was to become of her life when her money ran out.

THE MORNING AFTER HER BIRTHDAY, Catherine wandered along the streets once again. Hearing the church bells ringing had drawn her from her sleep and her room. She'd not even realized it was Sunday, and she'd hurried to dress and comb her hair back. She'd tucked it under her best bonnet and then donned her Sunday shoes. She hadn't been to a traditional church service since she'd left school, only the funeral for her family members, and she had a sudden desire to hear a choir sing and be surrounded by people once again.

She walked up the steps of the Congregational Church. It was a fairly new building and one that she knew nothing about, but she sensed an atmosphere of peace as she climbed the steps to the front doors. Peace was what she needed in her life at the moment, so she pushed any misgivings she might have aside and slipped through the doors just as they were being closed.

"Good morning," an older gentleman greeted her with a whisper.

"Good morning."

"Service is just beginning; can I help you find a seat?"

"No thank you. I'll just sit in the back pew. If that's alright?" Catherine asked timidly, feeling very out of place.

"Miss, you are welcome to sit wherever you wish."

"Thank you." Catherine stepped inside the large cathedral and slid onto the wooden seat of the last pew. A small choir of children was singing and she listened for a moment, the melodic sound pleasing to her ears and bringing a soft smile to her face. She closed her eyes as the music washed over her soul, rejuvenating her spirit in a way only music had ever been able to.

Since she was a little girl, she'd had music lessons of one sort or another. While her voice wasn't unpleasant, it had been decided by her music teachers that her real talent lie in her ability to play music on the piano, rather than her ability to sing. Catherine loved to play and she felt her chest tighten at the memory of her beloved piano, burned along with everything else in her family home.

The small group of children sang several songs, and then the congregants were invited to stand and join them. Catherine joined in as much as she could, and then she listened as a preacher talked about being steadfast and pressing onward, but rather than feeling bolstered by the message, she found herself with more questions.

*Steadfast in what? What am I supposed to be pressing on towards?*

The service ended an hour later and Catherine quickly made her way outdoors into the blinding sunlight, wandering down the street, her heart no lighter than before. She found herself standing in front of the library and wished she could go in and lose herself in a story for a while. But it was Sunday, and the library was not open on this day.

Sighing, she kept walking, watching people as they went about their day. Families having a picnic under then bright sun. Young men and women going here and there, arm in arm, completely unaware of how quickly their worlds could come crashing down.

But Catherine knew. All too well.

She found herself back in the park. She chose a bench looking out towards the river again. She was sitting there, contemplating her life, when an elderly woman sat down next to her and gave her a smile.

"Good afternoon," the woman told her, the voice husky from age. She was dressed commonly, and her hands were stained and weathered from working too many hours in poor conditions, but her smile was genuine, content.

"Good afternoon. Lovely day," Catherine told her and the woman nodded, smiling warmly.

Catherine tried not to become despondent over the fact that she was wearing a fashionable dress and overcoat, while the woman wore a drab dress and apron, yet the woman most likely had a family, home and a job waiting for her someplace in the city. Catherine's attire might indicate she had more than the woman, but in reality, the woman was likely much richer than she.

"That it is." The woman gazed out over the river, then turned back to Catherine. "Miss, you don't happen to know how to read, do you?" the old woman asked.

Catherine smiled at her, "Why yes, I do. Did you need something read to you?" she asked kindly, feeling a small sense of purpose arise within her as she sat up straighter.

"I have a letter from my daughter, but I'm afraid I can't read it. Would you be so kind?"

"Why, I'd be happy to." Catherine waited while the woman withdrew a stained and crinkled envelope from the apron tied around her waist. She smiled and then carefully unfolded the yellow parchment. She cleared her throat and then read, in a soft melodic voice -

*Dear Mama,*

*I hope this letter finds you in good health and spirits. I am doing fine here in Texas. Mr. Blakely and I seem to be getting along very well. We were married last Tuesday when the traveling magistrate came through town.*

*It was a simple ceremony, witnessed by two men from the saloon, but I didn't mind overly much. There's not much else here right now, and the only other women in town are the ones you wouldn't want me associating with.*

*Now that we're legally married, I no longer reside in a room above the saloon; I have moved to Mr. Blakely's ranch to live. I love it here. Open spaces. The weather is perfect this time of year. And Thomas — I call him that now that we're husband and wife — said you and Pa are welcome to visit anytime you like.*

*I'll try to write more often, but the nearest post office is half a day's ride away from the ranch. Don't fret if you don't get another letter from me for a while. I'll write when I can.*

*I love you mama. Tell Pa hello and that he can quit worrying about my safety. Becoming a mail order bride was the best thing for me. I hope to see you someday soon.*

*Love,*

*Sarah*

The woman clasped her hands over her mouth, tears shining in her eyes. "Oh, thank you! I've been so worried about that girl of mine since she boarded the train a month ago."

"Ma'am? What did she mean by mail order bride?" Catherine asked.

"Well, Sarah never wanted to do things the normal way." The woman laughed and shook her head simultaneously. "She got into her head that she wanted to see the frontier, but being female, her options for doing so were a might limited. She saw an ad about becoming a mail order bride. A real wife to some lonely man in the west. There aren't enough women out west, you see."

Catherine nodded her head, pretending to follow exactly what the woman was telling her.

"Sarah didn't have a beau here. Was a bit of a tomboy, that girl, and seems the boys here wanted refined, feminine-type ladies. Like you." The woman smiled at Catherine lest she offend her. "Anyhow, Sarah sent off a response letter to the man that placed the ad before either her Pa or I could stop her."

"What happened after she wrote to him," Catherine asked, genuinely interested in how this Sarah's eventual marriage had unfolded.

"That Mr. Blakely she writes about wrote her several letters and then he sent her the money for a train ticket and asked her to come be his wife. Just like that. I tell you, I've never heard of such a thing, and we did try to talk Sarah out of going, but she was determined. Stubborn as a mule sometimes, that girl of mine."

"She sounds very happy," Catherine commented, envying the unknown girl for knowing what she was doing with her life and having the courage to go after it.

"I'm glad for it now, after you read me her letter." The woman took the envelope and letter back and placed them reverently back in her apron. "My Wallace and I have been worried sick, wondering if she was well. Thank you again."

"You are very welcome." As the older woman prepared to walk away, Catherine called her back, "Excuse me, but where did your daughter find the ad?"

"The newspaper. There's an entire newspaper that has nothing in it but men out west who want to get married. Of course, there are some ads posted by the women themselves, but most of the ads are by men."

Catherine digested this piece of information and then asked, "Where would I find such a paper?"

"Try the post office. That's where my Sarah found a copy."

"I'll do that, thank you. Have a nice day."

"You too dear. Thank you again." The woman shuffled away, then turned back. "And good luck."

Catherine smiled and waved to the woman as she walked away and a plan began to form in her brain. If this

Sarah person could become a mail order bride and live happily ever after, why couldn't she do the same thing?

Becoming a bride sounded a whole lot better than taking a job in a rendering plant or sewing factory, the only two jobs that had turned up from her initial search. She stood up and made her way to the post office with a determined step. The office would be closed today, but there were always things posted outside on the wall of the building. As she made her way across the park and down three blocks, she silently prayed that this would be the answer she was seeking.

## 2

Catherine stepped into the post office and greeted the postman with a smile. "Good morning, Mr. Towner. Have you any mail for me?"

She had been visiting the post office every day for the last two weeks, and although she sensed the postmaster was becoming annoyed by her daily inquiries, she tried to remain positive.

"Today must be your lucky day." He peered at her over the top of his glasses that were perched halfway down his nose. "I have a letter right here for you." The postman retrieved a letter in a brown envelope and handed it to her with a smile.

"Thank you," she told him, her eyes trained upon the letter and what this could mean for her future. This was the second correspondence she'd gotten, and she hoped it meant she was on her way to leaving St. Louis in the near future.

After hearing about Sarah and her luck as a mail order bride, Catherine had visited this very post office and found a copy of the *Matrimonial Times* lying in a stack of discarded papers next to the building.

She'd picked it up and hurried back to her room, where she'd poured over each and every ad. She'd finally found the one that appealed to her the most –

*Single man, age 27, looking for a wife of some means to join me at the Arkansas-Texas border. I operate a small mercantile shop here. We just got the railroad a few months ago and business is growing quickly. Need a wife who isn't afraid to invest her money or her time in making this shop the biggest one in the county.*

*Must be fair of face and no older than 22 years of age. Prefer that she is educated, and has no vices.*

*Interested parties may write to me at Texarkana Post Office. Please enclose a picture of yourself when replying.*

*Mr. Samuel Cardwell*

Catherine had written a letter that same day and the next morning sent it off with a picture of herself taken while at school back East. She liked the thought of running a mercantile shop in a bustling railroad town that was not so far away. It certainly sounded better than some of the other ads for brides offered, like raising the five children aged 2 to 10 of a recent widower, or crossing Indian territory to settle in a mining town, or helping a new homesteader to build his own home before they'd have a roof over their heads. Since she still had a little bit of money left, she was confident this might be the place for her to make a new life. To start again and put the sorrow of the last few months behind her.

The gentleman who had placed the ad had identified himself as Samuel Cardwell. He hadn't included a picture of himself in the ad but she wasn't worried. Catherine had never put much stock in a person's looks, and as long as he was a kind and fair-minded man, she didn't care what he looked like. She'd written him a very pleasant letter and then waited for his reply –

Mr. Cardwell,

I saw your ad in the Matrimonial Times and would like to apply for the position of becoming your wife. I am a woman of limited means, but that was not always the case. I grew up in a very financially secure home and due to circumstances beyond my control, I now find myself in need of a fresh start. I would be willing to invest what I have in a new venture such as yours, a partnership if you like.

I have heard good things about both Texas and Arkansas; I look forward to seeing them both with my own eyes.

As for your list of requirements, I have enclosed a picture of myself, taken while away at school last term. I have just turned nineteen, and have been told that I play the piano beautifully. My singing voice will not ever be heard on a stage, but it is pleasant enough.

My parents saw that I had a good education, and I can read and write very well and can do my numbers as well. I am confident that this will serve me well in helping to manage a mercantile.

I hope this letter finds you in good spirits and I await your response.

Miss Catherine Lamott

The initial response she'd received from him had asked about her family, and she'd written a short reply about her father's illness and how it had spread. Samuel Cardwell specifically wanted to know about any extended family, grandparents or cousins and such, and she'd sorrowfully informed him she was entirely alone in this world. Both of her parents had lost their parents at an early age, and aside from her now deceased younger sister, she had no other siblings. She was now an orphan in this world, albeit a young woman.

She could see from the now-familiar penmanship on the envelope that this was another response from Samuel Cardwell and she was nervous with anticipation to read it. She hurried over to the park where she could read the letter in peace and quiet. She took a moment to reflect on the neat script that included her name and address. She liked that the man had such neat handwriting, and hoped that he had included a picture of himself. She hadn't asked for one, and now was wishing she had. She truly wished to put a face to the words that had been written.

She slipped her finger beneath the flap of the envelope, nudged it open and withdrew a single sheet of paper –

*Miss Lamott,*

*I enjoyed reading your first letter, and must say your second letter brought tears to my eyes. You are a lovely young woman and I appreciated receiving your picture just as much. I'm sorry that you've had such suffering recently and hope that this letter will bring a smile to your face and hope to your heart.*

*I especially like the fact that you have had schooling and would be more than capable of assisting in the mercantile with the bookkeeping and handling customers. And with schooling our children when the time comes. I would like to have a big family at some point in the future, and while I too am alone in this world and without any relatives to speak of, I believe we could become each other's family.*

*I am afraid that we do not have a piano here as of yet, but if you decide to become my wife, I will do everything in my power to see that one is brought to town so that you may delight us all with your talent.*

*The train now comes directly from St. Louis to Texarkana. If you still desire to become my wife after reading this letter, I would invite you to come to Texas. I have enclosed a small contribution towards your transportation and hope you understand that the bulk of my fortune is now invested in our future business.*

*Please let me know if and when you will be arriving. I am leaving the choice in your hands. If you come here to become my bride, I promise you will not be disappointed. I await your reply.*

*Mr. Samuel Cardwell*

CATHERINE WAS SMILING when she finished reading the letter. She held the shiny coin he had sent in her palm, turning it over a few times. It would not cover the entire cost of the trip, but she had sufficient money to pay for the ticket. *He wants me to come to Texas!* This was what she'd been hoping for. A purpose for her life and a chance to start again. She was tired of the looks from people who used to stop and talk with her, but now crossed to the other side of the street like she was a leper. She was tired of being alone all the time.

This was a chance for her to control her own destiny and before she could change her mind, she headed back to the post office.

"You're back," Mr. Towner said flatly.

"Yes. I need to send another letter. Do you have paper and a pencil I could borrow?"

"Sure do, miss." He slipped off the stool and shuffled to a

shelf behind the counter where he licked a finger to grab a single piece of stationery, then selected a stubby pencil, looking at it closely through myopic eyes to see that it still had a writing point. He handed her both items.

"You'll be wanting an envelope too, I imagine." he added.

"Yes, please," she said.

Catherine stepped aside to the counter where she would have space to write her response.

*Mr. Cardwell,*

*Thank you for your kind reply. I am looking forward to seeing Texas with my own eyes.*

*I will be purchasing a ticket to Texarkana and departing St. Louis within the week, but I do not know precisely when I will arrive. I will look for you first at your mercantile store, and in the event I do not find you, I will ask someone in your town for help.*

*I will be bringing my belongings with me, and if things work out, I will be willing to marry you immediately.*

*I look forward to seeing your store and possibly my future.*

*Miss Catherine Lamott*

SHE RE-READ what she had written three times and, satisfied, folded the parchment and placed it inside the envelope. She took a deep breath and then offered up a silent prayer that she was making the right decision. She was taking a huge leap of faith and hoped that Texarkana was where her future happiness lie.

## 3

T *exarkana, Texas 1881...*

RANCHER JACKSON TRIMBLE RODE into Texarkana and headed for the mercantile straightaway. Two men were sitting on the front porch and he nodded to them before entering the building. He gave his supply order to the proprietor, Mrs. Smythson, and then headed back out to the porch to wait while his order was gathered up.

Jackson had a cattle ranch about five miles outside of town, and since his housekeeper and ranch foreman had decided to get married and head West to search for gold, he was having a troublesome time keeping everything done, between the ranch and the house.

Mary had kept his house in order, taken care of the chickens and the milk cow, and acted as the cook for he and his men. She'd also seen to his laundry and had tended the vegetable garden out behind the house.

She had only been gone a week, and already he was out of clean clothes to wear, the storehouse was in complete disarray, and he and his men hadn't eaten a meal that wasn't either burned or raw in days. He'd finally had to send his men off to see about the fences and cattle, so he could come to town, restock supplies, and try to get things situated to his liking once again.

He'd done his laundry, it was now hanging on the line out back to dry, and he hoped he'd get back to the ranch before it got too dark. He'd made a list of the food items they were running low on, the list that Mrs. Smythson was now gathering, and he'd promised his men he would do his best to find them another cook. At this point, he didn't care if it was a man or a woman, although his chances of finding a woman willing to live at the ranch were slim to none.

His new ranch foreman, Shorty Jones, had jokingly told him the only way he'd convince a woman to live at the ranch was if he married her or kidnapped her. Since Jackson was a law abiding citizen, he'd discounted both choices. There were no single females living in Texarkana, unless you counted the loose women who worked at May's Place, and Jackson didn't.

He looked at the two disagreeable men sitting on the porch, wondering why they insisted on wasting their days away, seemingly doing nothing. Samuel Cardwell and Buster Young were both in their fifties, with scruffy gray hair, unkempt beards and clothes that looked like they hadn't been washed in months. There was always either a cigarette or a toothpick hanging out of their mouths and they got their entertainment by spitting onto the dirt street at precisely the moment a well-dressed passerby walked in front of them. They would laugh and if the passerby dared to question them, would stare back with such menacing eyes that the person would quickly lower their head and move along. That would start their laughing all over again.

They lazed their days away this way, offending upright citizens with their callous remarks and uncouth behavior, then spend their nights in the saloon, drinking and gambling. They didn't work as far as he could tell, and it was rumored that they had connections to several outlaws in the area. Jackson tried not to listen to rumors, but the men seemed to have enough cash to live on, and yet they never worked for it. That seemed suspicious to him.

Jackson had hoped that when the Texas Rangers started making Texarkana part of their normal route, the two men would clean up or move along to another town. But so far, neither of those wishful actions had occurred.

Not wishing to get drawn into a conversation with them, Jackson walked to the opposite side of the porch and leaned against the support beam, enjoying a smoke of his own. His supply order was rather large this time so would likely take Mrs. Smythson some time.

Jackson was making a mental list of the chores he still needed to get accomplished when he got back to the ranch, when the whispered conversation between Samuel and Buster caught his attention.

"She's acomin' here. Her letter was sent three days ago, so I'm a thinkin' she could be on today's train."

"Samuel, I still think you're takin' an awful risk. What if she don't play along and turns you in to the law?"

"She ain't gonna get the chance. When she shows up here looking for Samuel Cardwell, mercantile owner, I'll be waiting to take her to him and then we'll take a little walk. If she's nice, maybe I'll keep her around for a while. If not, then she'll be investin' in my future, if you get my meaning. If she cooperates,

I'll take her to the next town and put her on a train home. Otherwise, she just might end up meetin' her own demise."

"What if her folks come lookin' for her?"

"She ain't got no folks! Her last letter told the entire sorry tale. Her Pa got sick and gave his illness to her Ma and sister. They all died while she was away at some fancy school back East."

"I still say you're gonna get caught. They'll hang you fer sure."

"Nope. I aint' gonna get caught. She'll be too embarrassed by what happened to go to the law. And if'n she does, I'll be long gone with her money. Thinkin' about trying my luck down in Mexico."

The train whistled in the distance and Jackson turned to the side to see Samuel grinning and rubbing his hands together in glee.

"Now, remember if she shows up today, I ain't Samuel Cardwell, but I can take her to him. She thinks I'm 27."

Jackson was on high alert and suspicious of what the men had planned. If he'd heard correctly, Samuel had lured some young lady to come here and he was planning to steal her money when she arrived. He could only imagine how he had convinced her to travel here in the first place. He wanted to choke the life from the man. It was men like this that kept the west off limits to respectable women and families. No wonder it was so hard to attract good folks to this part of the country.

Jackson wondered if there was anything he could do. If this young lady was on the train, her very life could be in danger.

The Texas Rangers were providing the law for Texarkana while a new sheriff was found. The old one had been shot a month prior, just as the one before him. Texarkana was a fairly new town, and the criminals who'd been using it as a place to hideout were not happy with the progress being made to grow the small town. The expansion of the train meant that they were well connected all the way to the Mississippi river and beyond. Most of the townsfolk thought more law was needed to keep everyone in line, a move that was causing the outlaws to take more risk before there was a crack down and they'd either be jailed or forced to move on.

Unfortunately, Jackson knew for sure that the Rangers wouldn't be coming back through the area for at least another week. A recent train robbery had them in hot pursuit of a band of outlaws they had been chasing across Arkansas and Texas, all the way down into Louisana. They had pushed them into Texas now, and weren't stopping until the men were caught and brought to justice. If Jackson knew this, then no doubt so did Samuel and Buster.

Jackson saw it as his duty to step in and protect this unsuspecting female if she turned up, but he didn't want to get shot in the process and both Samuel and Buster were rumored to be quick on the draw. Jackson was quicker, but that was a part of his past that he had put behind him, and he really didn't want to resurrect it. He'd left his life of gun fighting behind him. He was a cattle rancher now.

*But this innocent woman has no idea of the danger she's in.*

Before he could decide if, and how, he should act, a soft voice called to the men on the porch of the mercantile.

"Excuse me, but I'm looking for Mr. Samuel Cardwell."

## 4

J ackson turned and sucked in a quick breath. Standing at the bottom of the steps was a lovely, petite young woman. She was dressed in a pristine white gown with long sleeves and a ribbon of black satin around the tiny expanse of her waist. Rather than a bonnet, she wore a matching stylish white hat atop her dark red hair. She had a smooth as cream complexion and large, deep brown eyes that looked so hopeful. Jackson hated knowing that before the afternoon was through, they would no longer sparkle with that same hope.

Samuel tipped his hat to her and stood up from the rocker he'd been lazing on. "Afternoon, ma'am. Samuel's at his house but he asked me to keep a look out for you. I can take you to him." He flashed a grin that showed stained and missing teeth.

To her credit, the young woman did not flinch at the repulsive man, but merely nodded and said, "Yes, please. That would be so kind of you."

Jackson couldn't believe what was happening right in front of him. He took a step towards the two men and then paused when Buster moved his duster out of the way and discretely revealed his Colt. He met Jackson's eyes, challenging him to remain quiet and motionless until Samuel and the young woman walked away.

Jackson's fingers itched to put the man in his place, but he also didn't want to start a gunfight with two men in the town square. Not with this lovely young woman in harm's way.

He held up his hands and backed away. He deliberately turned his back on the situation, while moving his draw hand down to the Colt sitting at his hip. He kept his hand loose and leveled his breathing so that he could hear everything going on behind him.

He heard Samuel chatting away with the young lady about her train ride, and offering to carry the two suitcases she'd brought with her as he led her away.

"Mr. Trimble, your order's all boxed and ready to go. Do you want it loaded up or shall I have Jimmy drive it out to the ranch for you?" Mrs. Smythson asked from the doorway.

"That would be much appreciated. I need to go see Jeb over at the feed store and then I'll head home. Tell Jimmy to go on out there and if I'm not there before him, have him speak with Shorty. He'll show him where to unload everything."

"Fine. I'll send him on his way now and I'll put all this on your account."

"Thank you kindly, ma'am." Jackson took advantage of their exchange to make his escape from the porch, certain that Buster wouldn't follow.

As he passed by the man, he didn't miss the soft voice, "Mind your own business and we won't have a problem."

Jackson did not acknowledge the veiled threat. He stepped up into the saddle and turned his horse towards the feed store, making sure Buster saw his direction which was opposite to that of Samuel's and the girl. Although he wanted to rush to the young woman's aide, he dared not arouse suspicion with Buster and only hoped that by the time he circled back around, Samuel wouldn't have had time to do any real harm.

He got off his horse at the feed store and entered the building by the front door, then in quick strides walked directly through and out the back door.

"Jackson, good to see you," Jeb greeted, his words fading as Jackson was through to the opposite door before he'd even finished saying them.

The shop owner came out from behind his counter and followed after Jackson nearly at a run, so unaccustomed as he was to seeing the younger man so impolite. "Jackson? What's gotten into you?"

"Samuel Cardwell is a lying, conniving snake and he's got a young woman...I don't have time to explain. Grab your rifle and catch up."

Jeb raised a brow, but stepped back inside and pulled down a rifle from the wall, "What are we shooting?"

"Vermin." Jackson made his way around the back of the building, keeping to the tall grasses and listening closely for signs that the young woman was in distress.

When they got closer to the back of the mercantile, he clenched his jaw and then paused to listen for a moment.

"What do you mean, you are Samuel Cardwell? Samuel Cardwell is 27. He said so in his ad. And he owns the mercantile. I don't understand any of this."

"You will. Now, you said you were willing to invest in our future. Just how much money are we talking about?"

"I'm not telling you anything until you take me to the real Samuel Cardwell."

"He is the real Samuel Cardwell," Buster's voice entered the conversation. "Now, be a good girl and dig your investment money out of them suitcases."

"I will not!"

The sound of a pistol being cocked was all the incentive Jackson needed to act. He moved forward quickly, both of his pistols in his hands and at the ready.

A scream of outrage and the sounds of a tussle reached his ears just as he broke through the grass. "Stop right there!" He raised his pistols, keeping one trained on each man. "Let go of her, Buster!" When the man failed to act quickly enough, Jackson pulled back the hammer on the gun he currently had trained on the man's forehead and issued another command in a low, deadly voice, "Now!"

"Don't listen to him," Samuel urged his cohort, having failed to draw his own pistol in time.

The sound of a rifle being cocked drew Samuel's attention, "What are doing involved in this, Jeb? Go away!"

"Now, Samuel. You know I can't do that. And just for the record, I'd listen to Jackson. The rumors haven't made it this far across Texas, it being such a big place and all. But Jackson's known for his gun fighting skills on the other side of the state. Ain't no one challenged him and lived to tell the tale."

Samuel and Buster both blanched at that warning and Buster released the young woman, shoving her away from him and causing her to fall to the ground.

Jackson kept his eyes on the two men, but asked her softly, "You alright, ma'am?"

"I believe so," she answered, although her shaky voice belied her assertion.

"Fine. You head on back to the mercantile store and find

Mrs. Smythson while these two gentlemen and I have a talk."

"But...my luggage..."

"I'll bring it along. Head on now. Get to the mercantile and stay inside until I come and find you."

He heard, rather than saw, the young woman pick herself up off the ground and rush back towards the mercantile. He waited until he was sure she was gone before he motioned Buster to join Samuel.

"Now, boys, this is what is going to happen. I do believe I heard you mention something about heading to Mexico, Samuel? Well, that would be an excellent idea. In fact, I suggest you leave town immediately. Today even.

"If I see you near that young woman, or hear that you're been back in town, I will personally come after you and hand you over to the Rangers the next time they're through town. They won't hesitate to shoot you or even have a public hanging once they hear what you tried to pull on that unsuspecting young lady."

He met both men's eyes, seeing hatred and a promise of revenge in them, but also doubt that they could prevail in a confrontation with Jackson.

"Do I make myself perfectly clear?"

Buster nodded, as did Samuel.

"Good. Jeb, would you relieve these two gentlemen of their weapons. I don't believe they'll be needing them in Mexico."

Jeb nodded and hesitantly collected the men's weapons. Once he'd stepped back, Jackson motioned with the pistol in his left hand, waving it in the direction of the path out of town. "Off with you now. And don't be thinking about loitering around here to bid your farewells. Don't think anyone here is going to be sad to see you go." He pointed with his pistol a second time. "Mexico is that way. On you go."

Jackson and Jeb kept watch for nearly half an hour, making sure the men didn't try to come back to the town. Once they were sure the two men were gone, Jeb returned to the feed store with a promise to bring Jackson's horse to the mercantile shortly.

Jackson nodded his thanks and headed for the mercantile. He wasn't sure what he'd just gotten himself into, but now that he'd interfered, he would have to deal with the consequences.

## 5

Catherine stood just inside the door to the mercantile, shaking and trying not to give way to the tears that were bubbling to the surface. She needed a chance to figure out what had just happened, but being accosted by two strange men, and then having two other men arrive with guns drawn was almost more than she could bear.

She closed her eyes and leaned her back against the door, trying to calm her racing heart.

"Miss, can I help you with something?" a kind womanly voice asked her.

Catherine snapped her eyes open and took in the stout woman dressed in a calico skirt and white button up blouse. Her bonnet matched her skirt, and her greying hair was sticking out around her head.

"I'm sorry," Catherine began, looking over her shoulder, "that man told me to come back inside here and wait for him."

"What man, child?"

"Well," Catherine paused. *Which man indeed!* "He was tall, with blonde hair, and blue eyes..."

"Well now. That would be Jackson Trimble."

Catherine peered through the window of the mercantile, careful to stay out of site. Her heart was still pounding from the encounter with the men.

The woman took another step towards her, "Dear, you look like you've had a fright. Come with me and I'll make you a nice cup of tea. Can you tell me what has upset you?"

"That other man, Mr. Cardwell, and his friend were going to...well, I'm sure they were going to rob me, and what else I don't even want to imagine. Mr. Trimble came to my rescue."

Catherine heard the scrape of a chair and footsteps coming from a back room. An older gentleman came into the front of the shop, wiping his hands on a rag tied at his waist.

"Here now! What is this you're saying about Cardwell going to rob you?"

"Dear, this is my husband, Mr. Smythson. That would make me Mrs. Smythson." She turned towards her husband. "I was just going to make the dear a cup of tea."

Turning her attention again to Catherine, she said, "The tea will help calm you so you can tell us what happened."

Mr. Smythson nodded, "Good idea. Sounds like Samuel's up to no good once again. What's he done, little lady?"

Catherine's mind was spinning. "So, that old man with the missing teeth, he really was Samuel Cardwell?"

"That he'd be. How'd a nice respectable young lady like you get mixed up with the likes of him?"

Catherine buried her head in her hands. *How could I be so gullible?* This was all going to sound so unreal to these nice people. She looked up and tried to explain what happened to this kind elderly couple.

"I hadn't actually met him until this afternoon. He and I have been corresponding for the past month or more. I came out here on the train, at his invitation. He suggested I become his bride. He said he was a 27 year old bachelor who owned the mercantile and needed a wife and business partner to help him run it."

As she repeated the story, she realized how implausible it all sounded. She really must have been desperate and lonely to have considered taking a journey all this way based on a couple of letters. Why had she not contacted a solicitor or her father's banker to look into Samuel Cardwell on her behalf?

"Good Lord, child! You don't want to get mixed up with the likes of him." Mrs. Smythson picked up the tea kettle that had started whistling and poured three cups of tea. "And he has never owned anything in his life. Mr. Smythson and I have owned the mercantile for near gone twenty years."

"I realize that now," she said sadly. "It was all a ruse to get me here so he could take whatever money and valuables I had with me."

"Why that no-good, rotten weasel!" Mrs. Smythson shook her head, hands on her hips. "Where is he now?"

"I'm not sure. Mr. Trimble and another man disarmed them and forced them to let me go. I was told to wait here where Mr. Trimble would deliver my bags after he had a talk with those scoundrels." Catherine wrung her hands. "I hope there is no violence."

Mrs. Smythson addressed her husband. "George, go see if Jackson needs help. He was heading to the feed store from here so Jeb is probably with him."

"If Jackson is handling things, it'll be just fine. He's one of the finest men I know around these parts." Smythson was not keen to enter into the fray if he could help it.

The bell sounded as the front door of the mercantile opened and all three of them turned to look in apprehension at the incoming visitor. Catherine exhaled in relief when she saw it was Jackson Trimble, each of his hands grasping one of her suitcases.

She rushed to him as the door closed behind him. "Thank you so much. I don't know what would have happened if you hadn't shown up."

"Well, I could probably hazard a guess and I can guarantee you wouldn't have liked the outcome. I brought your suitcases, Miss."

"Thank you," Catherine repeated.

"My dear, come sit down and drink your tea. Jackson, would you like a cup?"

Catherine found herself comforted by this stoic man's presence and hoped he would say yes to Mrs. Smythson's offer. He was tall and broad-shouldered and, although he seemed kind, there was something a little dangerous about him at the same time.

The older woman bustled to the bakery case and gathered a plate of sugary pastries to go with their tea as she and Jackson chatted away familiarly.

"...your name?"

Catherine looked up, startled, and blushed as she realized that Jackson Trimble had stopped speaking to Mrs. Smythson and asked her a direct question while she was deep in thought. "Sorry. What did you ask?"

"What is your name?"

"Catherine Lamott. From St. Louis, Missouri."

"That's a fair distance to travel. Mrs. Smythson tells me you'd been corresponding with Cardwell?"

"Yes. He placed an ad in the *Matrimonial Times* and I answered it."

"A mail order bride?" Jackson asked in surprise.

Catherine lowered her eyes as she felt the pink rise in her cheeks again at the humiliation of how she had been duped. "Yes."

Once she was able to put her embarrassment aside, she told the Smythsons and Trimble everything. About her parents and sister passing from the illness, the burning of their home and all their possessions. About her fiancé's decision to break their engagement once he discovered she was no longer wealthy. She told them about the creditors and business associates, and how none of the local towns-people, even those whom she thought were her friends, would come near her, afraid that she, too, was contagious with a deadly illness. By the end of it all, she was crying uncontrollably.

"I promised myself I was done crying, but this whole situation has ..."

"Of course it has," Mrs. Smythson told her, an arm around her shoulder, comforting her. "There, there. Now, don't fuss and make yourself sick. We have an extra bed and you are more than welcome to it until you can get the next train back home."

Catherine sighed, wishing she actually had someplace to call home. "Thank you, that is very kind."

Jackson sensed ambivalence from Catherine to the suggestion, despite it being the second time that day that she'd been rescued by strangers. "Miss Lamott, you don't seem happy about the idea of returning home."

Catherine shook her head and looked at him, "Mr. Trimble, do you have someplace to call home?"

Jackson nodded his head, "A cattle ranch five miles out of town. You call St. Louis home?"

"Not any more. I don't have anyone or anyplace to go back to. This was supposed to be a new start for me." She was quiet for a moment, furiously thinking about how she could fix the mess she'd landed in.

Looking up at Mrs. Smythson, she asked, "I don't suppose you carry the *Matrimonial News* here at the mercantile?"

"Can't say that I've ever heard of it, dear. But you can't be thinking of finding another man to marry through the paper?"

"I don't have many options. And I understand it works out for many women." Catherine gazed out the window, wistful as she remembered the woman who had received the happy letter from her daughter. But perhaps Mrs. Smythson was right and it was a risky notion. "When is the next train going back east coming through?"

"Not for another ten days."

"Oh," her face fell. She would burn through what money she had left in no time while waiting for the train. And then there would be the cost of the return ticket.

"You're welcome to stay with me and the missus until the train comes back." Mr. Smythson said gently. "Or until you figure out what you want to do." Mrs. Smythson smiled at her husband and squeezed his hand.

Catherine's eyes teared up at the kind gesture. "Thank you. That is very kind of you. I am able to pay for my room and board." Although she said this with confidence, she was not completely sure that she would be able to afford the train ticket after that.

"No, you most certainly will not! You'll stay here as our guest." Mrs. Smythson was adamant. They had their own daughter who was a bit older than Catherine. She had moved with her husband to Dallas some years back and Mrs. Smythson could only hope that were she ever in such trouble, a stranger would take kindly to her.

"Well, perhaps I can help you around the mercantile while I'm here?"

"Can you cook?" Mr. Smythson asked.

Catherine looked sheepish. "No."

"How about laundry and cleanin'?" he asked.

"No, but I'm sure I can learn," she said.

The Smythsons and Jackson looked from one to another.

Catherine added, "I've been attending university and am quite highly educated for a girl my age. My parents had help at home, so I was never taught to cook and clean."

Jackson did not wish to offend her, but had to ask what all three of them were thinking. "How were you planning to manage as a frontier wife without those skills?"

"I thought that I'd be helping Mr. Cardwell with the mercantile. I'm very good at arithmetic and bookkeeping, and can tend to the customers and the orders." Catherine became animated as she recalled her excitement at the life she had imagined that was not meant to be. She lowered her eyes. "I thought we'd have help to deal with the menial work."

Jackson could not restrain himself and guffawed loudly. This caused George Smythson to chuckle until Mrs. Smythson gave him a cautionary look to stifle his mirth and be compassionate.

"Dear, you must be tired. Let me show you to the extra room and you can rest before dinner." Mrs. Smythson ushered Catherine to the staircase, turning around and flashing a scowl at both her husband and Jackson for their insensitive outburst.

"Thank you. I am a little tired." Catherine picked up her suitcases and followed Mrs. Smythson up the steep staircase to the small rooms above. The Smythson's lived in their mercantile with the kitchen occupying the back of the stockroom, and their sleeping quarters above the store.

JACKSON WATCHED as Catherine disappeared up the staircase. When she was gone from view, he turned his attention back to George who was staring at him,

"What?"

"She's a pretty little thing, isn't she. And you heard her. She's looking for a husband. I saw the way you looked at her. Maybe you ought to consider gettin' yourself a wife."

"Wife? You heard her, she can't even cook. I need a cook and housekeeper."

George raised an eyebrow. "Looks to me like you need more than just a housekeeper. Cookin' and cleanin' can be learned. Unlike some other virtues." He could not hide the knowing smirk.

"There are other ways to get whatever else I need from a woman than marrying one." Jackson was not inclined to indulge in those ways, but he had no intention of continuing this line of conversation with Smythson.

But George was right about one thing. Jackson had been staring at Catherine. It had been a long time since he had laid eyes on a woman who took his breath away as she had done. Her red hair reminded him of ... no, he would not retrieve those memories.

Mrs. Smythson came back down the stairs, "Poor girl is plumb tuckered out. And that Samuel and Buster better never set foot on my porch again or I'll be taking daddy's shotgun to their behinds!"

"Miriam!" her husband said in shock.

"Don't you Miriam me! Those men should be horse-whipped for what they tried to do to that girl."

"Hopefully they won't be coming back anytime soon." Jackson tried to reassure Mrs. Smythson as he headed towards the door to be on his way. "I promised to hand them over to the Rangers if they ever set foot in town again."

Just as Jackson reached the front door of the mercantile, Jeb arrived and announced, "Jackson, your horse is tethered outside."

"Thanks, Jeb. Both for bringing the horse and for the assistance earlier."

"No problem. If they show up to cause trouble again, I'll help you corral them." Although Jeb in reality hoped to never find himself in a similar situation in future.

"I will," Jackson said and then shook hands with both Jeb and George Smythson. To Mrs. Smythson he tipped his hat as he put it on his head and exited the mercantile. "Thank you for the tea, ma'am. You take good care of that little lady."

He climbed up into the saddle of his horse and rode out of town, never realizing that a set of brown eyes watched him leave from the upstairs window, wondering if they would ever see him again.

## 6

"Catherine, why you don't go on up and change your dress?" Miriam Smythson suggested as they set the last loaf of bread on the counter to rise.

Catherine wiped her hands off on her apron and then looked down at her dress, "Why do I need to change my dress?"

"Well now, Jackson Trimble is coming by the mercantile today and I thought you might want to look your best."

*Jackson's coming here?*

"Why would I want to look my best for Mr. Trimble?" As nonchalant as Catherine attempted to sound, she was not fooling her older and wiser friend.

In the short time she had been staying with the Smythsons, Catherine had already learned a great deal from Miriam. Catherine had located a recent issue of the *Matrimonial Times* at the local library and had already responded to two of the ads for mail order brides.

One was a wealthy merchant in San Francisco whose family had made their fortune selling equipment to the miners during the California Gold Rush. He owned a mercantile as well as several boarding houses in the city and his ad said that he would send sufficient funds for a suitable, well-educated bride to have a comfortable journey west. The other was a lumberman near Seattle who was seeking a wife who would not be intimidated by the promise of life in a hectic, growing city.

George had promised to help her research the background of any suitor who responded positively before she made another journey. Miriam was teaching her basic cooking and housekeeping skills and she was rather enjoying it. She especially liked bread baking and how the dough became the fragrant, tasty warm loaf of goodness, fresh from the oven.

Miriam smiled at her now. Catherine wasn't fooling her with her aloof remark about a visit from Jackson.

"I believe he is coming by to check on your well-being and make sure you are getting along well," Miriam said. She then whispered, "You know there is no Mrs. Trimble."

Catherine's cheeks reddened.

Miriam could not keep quiet any longer. George had told her how Jackson had looked at Catherine, and the two had conspired to see if they could pull off a little matchmaking of their own. Part of this was having Miriam teach Catherine as much as possible about becoming a frontier wife, without her really suspecting.

"I happen to know that Jackson is looking for a wife," she said, although she realized that this wasn't exactly what Jackson had told George. "He needs a woman to make his ranch a home, but she'll need to be able to cook for not only Jackson, but his men too. And take care of the laundry and cleaning."

Catherine put her hands on her hips. "So that is why you have been teaching me so much these past few days!"

She could not be angry at Miriam. She had enjoyed her time here thoroughly, and appreciated that she would need these skills in future, even if she found a husband who did not initially require them.

The two women laughed together. Miriam told Catherine, "Just keep an open mind. If he makes a proposal, promise me you'll consider it. Now run upstairs and change your dress, young lady."

Catherine did as she was told. As she was pinning her hair up, she realized she was humming. Could it be that Texarkana will become her home after all? She had come to care for the Smythsons as if they were substitute parents and she was already accustomed to the lay of the town, having become familiar with the library and post office. And she had met several of the local townspeople when they visited the mercantile. She rather liked this friendly town and realized that she had not thought about St. Louis at all for the past many days. And then there was Mr. Jackson Trimble.

*He is very handsome. Maybe my run of bad luck is over. Mrs. Jackson Trimble.*

She giggled as she descended the staircase.

"I'M TELLING YOU, Jackson, she's a quick study."

George and Jackson sat on the front porch of the mercantile sipping a ginger beer, waiting for the ladies to announce that dinner was served.

"I told *you*, I'm not looking for a wife," Jackson said.

He had more important problems to solve, like finding someone who could cook hearty meals for ten ranchers every day, before they all quit. He'd already lost three of his best men who'd been lured away to a competing ranch with the promise of clean accommodations and hot meals.

"I know you did." George sat up straight and set down his ginger beer. "But Miriam has come to think the world of Catherine. With our own daughter so far away in Dallas, it's like having her nearby. She's a hard worker, and she seems to like the town. She's got no place to go, poor thing. It's so sad to see her make those daily trips to the post office waitin' to hear from one of those scoundrels advertising for a bride. It's downright pitiful, I tell ya."

"Is she still planning to take the train back to St. Louis next week?" Jackson asked, trying to appear only mildly interested in Catherine's future.

"Don't know," said George. "I understand she can't afford the fare. Miriam told her she could stay with us until she got a response to the letters she sent out. She's a big help, I'll tell ya. Made a dozen good bread loaves yesterday that we sold at the mercantile. So's no hardship for us to let her stay a bit longer. But she'll have to find a permanent home sooner or later. Or earn the money she needs for that train back to St. Louis."

"Can she cook a meal?" Jackson asked. "Or just bake bread?"

"No, no, she can cook a meal, too." George was quick to sing Catherine's praises. "All on her own last night she served us a stew. The meat darn near melted in your mouth."

Jackson was thoughtful and wondered if Miriam had taught her to do laundry and clean as well. Perhaps he could keep an open mind where Catherine was concerned.

∽

"YOU LOOK LOVELY, DEAR," Miriam said when Catherine came back to the kitchen. "Shall we call the men to the dinner table?"

Catherine had butterflies in her stomach as she stepped onto the porch behind Miriam. She heard Jackson's deep tenor voice as he was telling George about the activities at the ranch before she saw him.

"We've already arranged for one hundred steer to be moved ....," his voice trailed off as he became aware that the women had joined them.

"Miss Lamott."

"Mr. Trimble."

"You are looking well. I hear you've been learning to do all manner of things," he told her with a twinkle in his eyes.

Catherine nodded, tongue-tied for the first time in her life. She finally found her voice, "Yes. Miriam has been wonderful, teaching me all sorts of things."

*What was wrong with her? Surely she could do better than that.*

Sensing her charge's nervousness, Miriam invited them all to the dining room where they indulged in roasted chicken, creamy mashed potatoes with gravy, green beans and home-baked bread with butter. Miriam persisted in telling Jackson that Catherine had cooked the entire meal and every time Catherine attempted to correct that fact, either George or Miriam would change the subject and blurt out some gossip from around town.

After they had finished eating the apple pie doused in fresh cream, another one of Miriam's concoctions that was credited to Catherine, George yawned and stretched.

"I'm going to call it a night," he said. "Early day tomorrow." His attempt to discretely leave Jackson and Catherine alone was so obvious they all recognized the charade and giggled simultaneously.

Jackson decided to let the Smythsons have their way. "Miss Lamott, would you care to take a stroll with me to walk off that delicious meal? I fear my horse will be weighed down by the extra pounds. It was scrumptious." He held his hand out to her.

"Thank you." Catherine had stopped trying to deny that she'd cooked the meal since Miriam was so set on convincing Jackson otherwise. She accepted his hand and stood up to join him. "A walk sounds lovely."

As they walked, Jackson asked her how she was enjoying her time with the Smythsons. At dinner with the four of them together, Catherine had already been forthcoming with Jackson about her responses to the mail order bride ads on the west coast, and that she was ambivalent about taking the return train to St. Louis.

"Miriam tells me you're a quick learner. She couldn't say enough nice things about you. You've made quite an impression on her and George." Jackson clasped his hands behind his back as he walked.

"They're such nice people. I don't know what I would have done if they had not let me stay with them while waiting for the train to come back through."

"I've known them for a good long while, and I trust their judgment as well." He was quiet for a moment as they reached the end of Main Street and he paused before leading her back the way they had come. "They both think you and I might be a good fit together. That we each have something to offer the other that could solve both our problems."

Catherine looked at him from beneath her lashes and was amazed to see him watching her so intently. She swallowed hard, her neck felt flushed and her palms were sweaty. She was too nervous to speak. *Miriam was right. I can't believe this is happening.*

Jackson took the cue that, with her silence, Catherine was waiting for him to continue with his proposal.

"I understand you may not be taking the train back to St. Louis just yet." he said. "But George says you quite like our town. That you are finding it ... *homey*?"

She smiled, "Yes." Her voice caught in her throat. *Just come out and ask me!*

"I know that living away from the city, in the frontier, wasn't exactly what you came here for."

"No ..."

"As you know, I have a ranch," he said. "It's not so far from town that you could not visit frequently. And the landscape is breathtakingly beautiful. Most people who see it love it immediately, and cannot imagine living away from nature."

"It sounds wonderful," she said, her voice quickening, breathless.

"So I was wondering ..." Jackson stopped walking and turned to her. He gazed intently into those deep brown eyes, searching. "Miss Lamott, would you be interested in moving to my ranch to become my cook and housekeeper?"

## 7

Catherine hurried upstairs and shut her bedroom door before flopping face down on the small bed and, with her head buried in the pillow, sobbed with labored, heaving breaths. It had been all she could do to walk the rest of the way back to the mercantile with Jackson and say her goodbyes while keeping her composure.

She almost didn't hear the faint knock on her door.

"Catherine, dear." It was Miriam. She must have been listening for her return, curious to discover what she and Jackson had spoken about.

"Go away," Catherine said. She was too humiliated to talk to her friend.

Miriam heard the distress in the younger woman's voice and was not to be denied. She opened the door softly, then ran to the bed when she saw Catherine lying there, wracked with grief.

"Oh my dear, what happened?"

It took some minutes before Catherine was able to compose herself, sit up, and tell Miriam about Jackson's proposal. "He wants to hire me to be his housekeeper and cook. He doesn't want a wife!" And then she collapsed, totally mortified, all over again.

Once Miriam had settled Catherine and convinced her to get some sleep and take a fresh look at her situation in the morning, she scolded her husband for not ensuring that Jackson proposed marriage rather than employment.

"You cannot blame me, Miriam," George bemoaned. "I did my best to steer him the way you wanted. I told him how much she had learned about cookin' and cleanin'. He said he didn't want a wife."

"Well, you best get out to the ranch tomorrow and have a talk with that man," she said. "He broke that girl's heart, not to mention, embarrassed the poor thing."

"Yes, dear."

"What brings you out this way, George." Jackson and his foreman, Shorty, were just closing the gate to the corral to keep the cattle contained when Smythson rode up in his wagon.

"Brought out those bushels of apples and potatoes you ordered. Came in a day early." George was glad he'd found an excuse to journey all the way out to Jackson's ranch from town.

"Mighty kind of you, George, but there was no need to do that. I could've picked them up when I came to town tomorrow." Jackson moved swiftly between the corral and the barn then around to the side of his house and started to split firewood. There was never a moment to spare on the ranch and Jackson was an expert at making every minute count.

"Say, Jackson," George said as he took off his hat and scratched his head. "I hear you offered the young lady a job."

"Yep."

"To be your cook and housekeeper."

"Yep." Jackson looked up from his log-splitting. "You have a problem with that?" he asked. "Seeing as how you've taken the gal under your wing and all."

"Nope." George paused, not sure how to broach the subject that he felt was none of his and Miriam's business in the first place. "It's just that ... well, we sorta hoped you might consider marrying her. Seeing as how she's looking for a husband and all." He couldn't help but mimic Jackson's own phrasing.

"Listen, George, I told you that I wasn't looking for a wife," Jackson replied. "And just because that girl is willing marry someone she barely knows ... hell, she was willing to take a train across the country to marry someone she never met! But that doesn't mean I would marry a woman only a week after meeting her, no matter how pretty she is or how good a cook."

"C'mon, Jackson," George pleaded. "You really think she's going to come out here and take care of the cooking and housework without the benefit of marriage? She's a respectable lady."

"And I'll treat her as one," Jackson said. "She'll have her own quarters, just like my last housekeeper, Mary. I'll pay her well and she can earn what she needs to buy her train ticket back to St. Louis. If that's what she wants."

He paused. "Who knows, maybe just like Mary, after a time, she'll find someone to marry her here as well." He winked and smiled at George, the meaning not lost on the older man.

"I can't blame ya, Jackson. Have to admit, I understand."
George had finished unloading the bushels of apples and
potatoes and climbed back into the wagon to head home.
Miriam wasn't going to be happy about the outcome. His
hesitation to go home and report the news back to his wife
must have been obvious to Jackson.

"I've made some mistakes in my past, George," Jackson
attempted to explain. "Mostly because I made decisions in
haste. Both in matters of the heart, and matters of the law.
I'm not going to make snap decisions ever again."

WHEN GEORGE RETURNED HOME, it was apparent that
Catherine had still not recovered from the perceived slight
that was Jackson's offer. She and Miriam sat at the kitchen
table sipping tea, glum looks on both women's faces.

Miriam brightened when George walked in. "Did you
speak to him?" she said.

George relayed the conversation he'd had with Jackson
and tried to soothe Catherine's hurt feelings.

"I can tell he cares for you, my dear," George said. "But
he is a deliberate fellow and does not come to life-changing
decisions lightly. I think you should accept his offer."

Both women straightened their backs and stared at
George, eyes wide.

"George!" Miriam exclaimed. "You do not really mean to
suggest that Catherine live with that man as an unmarried
woman. How disgraceful!"

George raised his hand to settle his wife down. "Now,
Miriam, hear me out. Jackson's last housekeeper, Mary, was
a single woman when she moved out there. You might
remember, her pa was a widower and after he passed, she

had nowhere to go. Jackson gave her her own private rooms and no one thought the worse of her for living out there as his housekeeper. That's where she met her fella."

Miriam turned to Catherine, "What do you say, dear? You've no better option for now."

"Couldn't I work for you? Here in the mercantile?" said Catherine, her bottom lip quivering.

"Oh, child, I wish you could," Miriam said. "But truth is, George and me, we're just barely getting by. With the train here now, rumor has it that another general store is being built just down the road and that will take some of our business. 'Specially since it will be closer to the homes along Oak Street."

George added, "I did get the feeling that Jackson wasn't totally against the idea of marrying you in the future. If things worked out and all."

"Oh hush, George," Miriam hissed. "Giving her false hopes is what got her feeling bad to begin with."

George sighed. "Well, then, I guess you'll just have to wait to hear back from one of them fellas out west lookin' for a mail order bride."

Catherine swallowed hard and Miriam shook her head at her husband to silence him. He had obviously made another blunder. He would never understand women and stood up to shuffle out to the front of the store and leave the two women in peace.

Miriam realized that her husband could not be expected to know his error, and explained gently. "Catherine received a reply from the one in San Francisco. He thanked her for her letter but said he had just married another girl. That was the one she really had high hopes for."

"Oh. Sorry to hear that," George said, and ambled to the kitchen door. He turned around and gave it one last try, certain that if Jackson and Catherine just had more time to get to know one another, that things would work out. "I still think you ought to consider Trimble's offer." With that, he left the women alone.

Miriam and Catherine sat silently at the table for several minutes. Finally, Miriam stood up and fetched the kettle from the stove. The water was still hot, so she added some to both of their tea cups.

"It's not a bad option." Miriam spoke softly, almost daringly.

Catherine nodded her head, nearly imperceptibly. She knew she had no other option. She could continue writing letters to men seeking a mail order bride. She could take her time and be choosy, not jumping at the first one that sounded halfway suitable. Or she could return to St. Louis once she'd earned enough money for the train fare. In the meantime, she would learn to cook, clean, do laundry and make a cozy home for Jackson Trimble. It would be good practice for when she finally met her future husband.

## 8

Catherine arrived at the ranch mid-day when the sun was high in the sky. The view from the porch surrounding Jackson's cabin was breathtaking, just as he described, with lush grass and green trees as far as the eye could see.

George had driven her to the property in his wagon with her meagre belongings because Jackson and Shorty were busy with a cattle run. Jackson had shown George where Catherine's rooms were located, safely on the opposite side of the cabin from Jackson's own. George showed her to a humble, but clean and spacious bedroom, just off the kitchen, that she would call her own for the time being. It was not as luxurious as the bedroom she'd grown up in, in her parents home, but she had to bury that thought. She was pleased to see a tiny separate sitting room attached to the bedroom with a desk and chair. Here she would write letters to potential suitors to apply to be their mail order bride. Although now she felt less urgency to find a husband quickly, and would take her time and be a bit selective in which ads she responded to.

George carried her suitcases into the room and placed them in the corner before bidding her farewell. "Don't be a stranger, young lady," he said. "Miriam has already told Jackson that she expects you both for Sunday dinner."

Catherine smiled at the gesture from the dear couple that had become such a big part of her life in a short time and stood waving goodbye to George from the porch until she could no longer see him.

Turning back inside the cabin, she decided she would unpack later. Right now she wanted to see the rest of the cabin before Jackson arrived home to get a sense of what she would be tackling if she had to keep it clean in addition to cooking for ten hungry men every day.

As she entered the comfortable living room with it's large stone fireplace, her eyes wandered to the opposite side of the room. She stopped and clasped her hands over her mouth to stifle a squeal of glee.

"A piano!"

Catherine ran to the large upright piano standing against the east wall of the living room and stood reverently in front of it. She slid the stool out from under the keys and lightly sat on its edge. She ran her hands across the gleaming wood and gingerly lifted the fallboard as she admired the beautiful instrument.

Her fingers brushed the keys tentatively, then struck one at a time in a familiar melody. In minutes, she was lost in the music, expertly playing Beethoven's Für Elise. It had been years since she last played, yet it came back to her as effortlessly as breathing.

When she finished, she was overcome with emotion and drew in a deep breath before closing the fallboard back over the keys.

"That was beautiful."

Catherine leapt to her feet in alarm. "Oh!"

She had not been aware that Jackson had walked into the cabin as she played.

"I'm sorry," she said. "I thought I was alone."

"No need to apologize," he said. "You play beautifully."

"Do you ... play?" she asked.

"No." He simply stated his reply with no explanation.

"But you have a piano." She lifted an eyebrow in a questioning gesture. "And I understood you lived alone."

"I once knew someone who played." Jackson turned to leave and then added, "I hope you find your accommodations suitable. Shall I show you the rest of the house and grounds now?

"You'll need to know where the larder and pantry are in order to plan and prepare the meals. I trust you will be happy to fetch the provisions from the mercantile each week. It will give you an opportunity to go to town to see the Smythsons."

"Yes, of course," she said, and scurried after him to keep up with his long strides as he headed toward the pantry.

The pantry and larder were quite well-stocked given that Jackson's trip to the mercantile had been less than a week earlier. Catherine was glad to see several of the familiar items that she'd already learned to cook with Miriam. In stock were flour and yeast for bread; onions, carrots and potatoes for a stew; apples to bake a pie; eggs and bacon for breakfast and several varieties of meat.

"Well, then, I'll leave you to it." Jackson seemed to always be in a hurry to move along to his next task as he escaped out the door.

Right. She might as well get started immediately, knowing a gang of hungry ranchers would soon expect a hot meal. She would unpack her bags and get settled in her room quickly, then start preparing the evening meal.

She'd had the foresight to purchase several ready-made frontier skirts and blouses before leaving St. Louis which she had been wearing at the mercantile rather than her fancier dresses. Miriam had been quick to tell her that working on a ranch was hard, sweaty, dusty work sometimes, and she might as well get used to getting her clothing dirty right from the start.

She'd already experienced some of that while helping Miriam with the cooking and cleaning around the mercantile. She'd covered herself in flour the first time she kneaded bread, and doused herself with water the first time she scrubbed the laundry. Her hands were already becoming chafed from the lye soap and hot dishwater and she made a mental note to purchase some soothing lotion from the mercantile as soon as she'd earned her first wage as a housekeeper.

By SUPPERTIME, Catherine felt as if she had a good handle on what her responsibilities would be at the ranch. There was a cow to milk and chickens to feed, and eggs to be collected each morning. She'd already learned that she only needed to prepare breakfast for Jackson. The men would have eaten before arriving for their day's work. But come late afternoon, she would be expected to put a hearty, warm, rib-sticking meal on the table for twelve people, herself and Jackson included.

The ranchers worked until sundown after that, then headed home to their own families for their late night meal.

But the hot supper Catherine cooked for them was their main meal of the day, so had to be filling.

"THANK YOU, MA'AM," echoed throughout the dining room as the men stood up to return to the field following their first meal prepared by Jackson's new cook and housekeeper.

The house held a long wooden table just off the kitchen, with two benches on either side, each one big enough for five burly ranchers. Jackson and Catherine sat at either end of the table. At first, Catherine tried to retreat to her room after serving the meal, but Shorty, Jackson's foreman, had insisted that she eat together with them.

"Mary always ate with us," he said. "Ain't that right, Jackson."

Jackson nodded, "You're welcome here at the table, Miss Lamott. We're just one big family here, and the men are used to minding their manners indoors. Mary insisted on it."

As Catherine sat down to share her first cooked meal with them, she announced boldly, "Well, if we're family, then you all might as well call me Catherine. It sounds like there was no formality when Mary was here, and I don't require it either."

That endeared her to the men and they all seemed to relax a bit easier as they dug into the pot roast that she'd served. She was relieved that it was edible and even noticed that the men were soaking up the gravy on their plates with corn bread. They ate every last morsel she had cooked and she made a note to prepare larger portions the following day. The men certainly had appetites.

Once the ranchers had retreated outside to continue their work, Catherine started the task of cleaning up the dishes. First she had to take the bucket outside and pump water which then had to be heated on the stove. She gathered the twelve plates, cups, forks and knives and once she had washed, dried and re-stacked them, started on the cast iron pot. After scrubbing for a good ten minutes, she decided to let it soak overnight to get the burnt bits off the bottom.

She swept the floor and when she was finally done, stepped out onto the porch to watch the sun slowly setting in the west. It was beautiful, but this vast wilderness also brought a loneliness with it. Catherine sat on the porch swing and wondered what would become of her. How long would she remain the cook and housekeeper on this ranch? Would she get a positive reply to any of her letters to men seeking a mail order bride? And would any of them result in a better outcome than her first attempt?

Exhausted, Catherine walked inside to her small bedroom, knowing that sunrise would come soon enough. It was best if she tried to get some sleep.

## 9

Catherine was starting to get a handle on the daily chores around the ranch and she woke up early, just as dawn peeked through the sky. Her first week was exhausting and her muscles ached with every move, but as each day passed, she could feel her strength and energy returning.

She needed to get her energy back. Since arriving at the ranch, she had not sent a single response to any of the ads in the latest issue of the *Matrimonial Times*, despite seeing one or two that caught her eye. When she awoke in the morning, she was in a rush to milk the cow, gather the eggs and make Jackson's breakfast before he headed out to the ranch, which he tended to do as soon as the sun came up. In the evening, by the time the dishes were cleaned and put away, the pots and pans washed, and the floor swept, she could hardly keep her head up or her eyes open. During the daytime, she was either doing laundry, baking or preparing meals.

On Sunday, Jackson had driven them both into town to have dinner with the Smythsons. Catherine had nearly begged off, so tired was she that she hoped to catch up on some much needed rest. But she couldn't bear the thought of disappointing George and Miriam and, truth be told, she also needed their companionship. It was lonely on the ranch and she often found herself talking aloud to no one at all.

She had hoped to play the piano occasionally when no one was around. Jackson had given her permission to do so. But she was even too tired for that.

"It is so good to see you, my dear," Miriam had said when Catherine climbed down from Jackson's wagon, giving her a bear hug and a kiss on both cheeks. "Come, let's have a cup of tea and you can tell me how you are."

Catherine was almost too tired to even tell Miriam how her first week had gone, and Miriam seemed disappointed when Catherine mentioned the recent interesting advertisements for brides that she hoped to respond to once she had time.

Catherine smiled as she recalled the older woman's disappointment. She knew that Miriam hoped that Jackson and Catherine would become more than just employer and employee. Catherine wasn't sure if it was as much for Catherine's sake as Miriam's own, knowing that the older woman thought of Catherine as a sort of substitute for her own daughter, so wished to keep her near by.

As she gathered the eggs, Catherine realized that she too was disappointed by Jackson's aloofness. When they first met, she thought he'd seemed fond of her. She found him to be a kind man with high moral standards. He was hard working and treated his men well. And her. Yet he was distant.

George and Miriam said they thought he suffered some tragedy in his past, but that no one in Texarkana knew what that was. They did reveal to her that he had been a lawman in west Texas some years back, with a reputation for being fair, but tough, on criminals. Rumor was that he left the law to take up ranching, but no one knew why.

Catherine spoke softly to the cackling hens as she moved from one nest to the other, collecting the fresh eggs. Once she'd collected a full basket, she exited the coop and then slipped through the gate to the yard without allowing any of the chickens or rooster to escape.

She walked around the backside of the coop and was just passing the large oak tree that gave shade to the yard, on her way back to the cabin, when an arm reached out from behind the tree and grabbed her around the waist.

She opened her mouth to scream, but a hand slapped over her mouth more quickly than she could expel a breath, and she was wrestled to the ground.

"Quiet, woman!" Samuel Cardwell had her pinned to the ground, one arm wedged under her waist and the other clasped over her mouth.

"We're going to get up real nice and easy, and I don't want to hear a peep out of you, ya hear?" His rancid breath nearly caused her to wretch as he removed his hand from her mouth.

"Help!!!! Jackson!!!!!!"

Samuel did not anticipate her feistiness and lost his grip, allowing Catherine to squirm away momentarily, swinging her basket of eggs wildly as she ran.

"Come back here you!" Samuel hollered, running after her.

She ran as fast as she could but the man was faster. He lunged at her and managed to grab her skirt and pull her off balance.

"Get away from me! Jackson! Shorty! Help!!!!" As she

stumbled to the ground and he was nearly upon her, she threw one egg after another at him, but he was not deterred.

Just as Catherine was sure she was within his grasp, Samuel Cardwell stopped cold in his tracks. Catherine heard the cock of a shotgun behind her.

"I thought I made myself clear." Jackson stood in front of Cardwell, shotgun aimed directly at the man's chest. The tone of his voice was calm but menacing. "You are not welcome in Texas. And you are certainly not welcome on my ranch."

"I ain't got no beef with you, Trimble," Cardwell had regained his composure and held his hands up in a gesture indicating he did not want any trouble. "I'm just here for what's rightfully mine."

"Oh? And what might that be?"

"I sent train fare for this little lady to come and be my wife and take care of me." He had a cocky smirk on his lips as he said the words. "I'm here to make good on that."

"Like hell you are." Jackson did not relax his stance with the shotgun one iota.

"Yeah, well, I can see why you would say that. I see you took her for yerself. But you didn't even offer to marry her. I'm willin' to make a respectable woman out of her."

"You deceived her and then attempted to rob her," Jackson said calmly. "We'll see what the Ranger says about that when he comes back this way."

Shorty arrived and Jackson told him to take whatever weapons Samuel Cardwell might have on him, then tie him up and lock him in the barn. They would keep him secure until he could be turned over to the authorities.

To Catherine, Jackson said, "I thought you were going to cook those eggs?" He pointed to the overturned basket, and the batch of broken eggs on the ground that she had thrown at Cardwell. He could not hide a cheeky smirk.

Catherine smiled and replied, "We had a few extras and I was of a mind to share."

Jackson laughed and said, "I think we better find you a proper weapon."

Despite the fright she'd had, Catherine felt surprisingly optimistic. Samuel Cardwell was in custody and would be turned over to the authorities. She could rest easy, no longer fearing some future retaliation. She also felt hopeful. The banter that she and Jackson had exchanged was the first lighthearted conversation they'd had since she arrived.

## 10

Catherine was up earlier than usual, having slept fitfully, knowing that Samuel Cardwell was still on the property. It could not be soon enough that the Ranger would be back in town to take him off Jackson's hands.

Worse yet, Catherine had to cook breakfast for the scoundrel every morning. Jackson had asked her to make an extra plate of eggs and bacon for him the first morning after he'd been locked up, and expected the same each morning since. It was not Jackson's way to mistreat anyone. Gratefully, she was not required to deliver the food to the prisoner; that duty was passed to Shorty.

As she served Jackson his breakfast and refilled his mug of coffee, she caught him staring at her. And he was smiling.

She had no idea how that man thought. One minute he was sullen and withdrawn, the next he was saving her from a fate she did not even want to imagine, the next he was insisting that a criminal eat as well as any of his men. Now he was smiling as he watched her in the kitchen.

Catherine found it all quite unsettling. More unsettling to Catherine were her own feelings. She imagined that her stint as a cook and housekeeper would be brief, while she earned money and took her time to find herself a suitable husband through the *Matrimonial Times*. But she found herself less interested in writing the letters, even as she regained her energy. Was it possible that she was starting to feel like this place was home?

JACKSON'S EYES followed Catherine as she moved around the kitchen, going through the routines that she'd settled into with greater ease than he had anticipated. He was surprised at his own feelings as he watched her. For one, pride. He was proud of the way she had tackled the work at the ranch, knowing that she came from a more refined background and was new to cooking and cleaning. He was also proud of how she rebounded from the experience several days earlier when Samuel Cardwell accosted her, obviously with intentions to do some serious harm to her. She was a strong woman, stronger than he initially assumed.

He smiled as he recalled her quip about the eggs. Was it only pride he was feeling? Did his feelings go deeper than that? He vowed that he would never let another woman into his heart again, but this one was certainly getting under his skin.

His thoughts were interrupted when Jimmy, one of the wranglers, knocked on the kitchen door.

"Boss, sorry to disturb."

Jackson wiped his mouth with a napkin and stood up. It was about time he got his day started. "What is it Jimmy?"

"Have you seen Shorty?" Jimmy asked. "He told the five of us wranglers to wait for him at the corral more than half an hour ago. Said he'd be right back, but we haven't seen him. Thought maybe he was with you."

Jackson had a bad feeling. "Last I saw him, he was taking a plate of grub down to the prisoner. Get Caleb and meet me down at the barn."

"Boss! Boss! Come quick!"

Jackson and Jimmy hurried out of the house as Tom, the assistant foreman came running, shouting and waving his arms, breathless.

"Shorty's hurt, bad!" Tom yelled. "Looks like Cardwell got hold of his pistol when Shorty took him his breakfast and shot him. He's unconscious and there's a lot of blood, but he seems to be breathing."

"Where is Cardwell?" Jackson snapped.

"Gone, boss," Tom said as the men moved with determined strides. "He managed to get loose of the shackles. Ain't seen no sign of him."

AFTER THE MEN rushed in the direction of the barn to tend to Shorty, Catherine stood on the porch, pale, uncertain, wondering what, if anything, she should do.

All she could think of was to fetch water and put a pot on the stove to boil. There was a good chance that they would need to tend to Shorty's wounds. She had seen some gauze and antiseptic in the kitchen. She would get that ready. She would make herself useful.

Catherine fetched the bucket that she used to fill water from the pump for washing the dishes and walked around the side of the cabin to fill it up.

"Ooh-wee, look what we have here."

Catherine froze.

"If it isn't my long lost fiancé." Samuel Cardwell smiled at her. His accomplice, Buster, stood right behind him.

## 11

Catherine started to scream, but Buster covered her mouth with his hand and it was all she could do to not retch, the smell was so vile. He pinned her arm to her side with his other hand as she squirmed to get away.

"You be quiet!"

"Get her to the horses. We need to get out of here before the ranchers come back."

Catherine was in a full panic. She didn't know where these men intended to take her, but she was quite certain that if they disappeared with her, she'd never see Jackson or Miriam or George again. She fought with every ounce of strength she had, even after Samuel slapped her across the face. Hard.

She tasted blood, but she still fought them as they dragged her towards the horses. When she kicked Buster in the shin, he momentarily loosened his hand and she bit him. As hard as she could.

He shoved her away from him and she screamed for all she was worth. "Jackson! Jackson! Help me!"

They were too far away from the house for Jackson or his men to hear her and she felt tears slide down her cheeks as she realized how helpless she truly was.

Samuel finally got tired of her fighting and he hit her again. This time she didn't even have time to cry out. She fainted from the pain, falling to the earth before Buster could catch her.

"Don't drop her! If Trimble finds out she's gotten hurt, he not only won't pay, but he'll never stop hunting us down." Samuel grabbed her arm before she could land face first in the hard packed dirt, ripping the shoulder seam of her dress in the process.

"Get her up on the horse and let's get out of here."

They flung Catherine onto a horse like a rag doll, kicked the beasts into a gallop and thundered away, dirt kicking up behind them.

In their haste, they did not see Jimmy, the young rancher, hiding behind the tree watching as they carelessly tossed Catherine across the saddle. He arrived too late to intercept them, but the least he could do was find out where they were taking her.

Jimmy had been sent back to the cabin at a run to have Catherine boil water and set out the medical supplies needed to patch up Shorty. The rest of the men were slowly carrying Shorty back to the house in a make-shift gurney, trying not to jolt him too much until they could get him to safety.

Jimmy followed Samuel and Buster, making sure he stayed far enough back so they could not detect him. Once he discovered the location of their camp, he hightailed it back to the ranch and told Jackson what had happened.

～

JACKSON WAS INCENSED. "Rangers or no rangers, I want those men. Dead or alive. It doesn't matter."

The men headed to the bunkhouse to grab their guns and extra bullets. Jackson had called upon them to help him hunt down the men who had kidnapped Catherine. He wanted justice and he intended to have it.

Every man had eagerly stepped up and Jackson was reminded how lucky he was to have found this group of men to work alongside him. They were loyal, not only to him, but to the notion of law and order, and fairness. That was about the best he could hope for. In addition, they had all taken an immediate liking to Catherine and would do anything to protect her.

As the sun rose higher in the sky, the group of men rode out in search of the young, innocent woman who Jackson had brought to his ranch as a cook and housekeeper, and who was now in mortal danger. He had not known her for long, but she had already stolen a piece of his heart, something he finally had to admit.

Jackson did a lot of thinking as they rode through the woods, Jimmy leading the way to the outlaws' camp. Catherine had been doing an amazing job as she tried to accomplish everything that a more experienced housekeeper might find challenging. Considering that she had not previously learned to cook or clean, nor had ever lived outside of a big city, he was impressed by the progress she had made.

As he rode in silence, he recognized a feeling in the pit of his stomach that he had not felt for a very long time. He had already admitted to himself that he was very fond of her. Was it possible that he was actually falling in love with her? He had offered her the job at the ranch to help her out, so she could earn the money she needed for train fare home after she had suffered at the hands of Cardwell. But in reality, he was not sure he was ready to see her leave Texarkana to be some other man's mail order bride. He wanted time to get to know her. To discover if they could have a future together, as man and wife.

Jackson also sensed something in her attitude, the way she hummed as she cooked, and smiled at him when she served his meals. Was it possible that she had feelings for him too?

One thing he knew. He would do everything possible to get her back safely, to free her from Samuel Cardwell's vile grip, if it was the last thing he did.

Jackson was no stranger to enforcing the law, to exacting justice. He no longer carried a badge with the authority to do so, but he was confident that he would not be held accountable should he not be able to bring Samuel and Buster back alive. Not after what they had done.

Although Jackson had discarded his previous life years ago to enjoy a more peaceful one living off the land, he had no problem resurrecting that part of himself if it meant getting Catherine back safe and sound. No problem at all.

## 12

Catherine was sweaty, thirsty, tired, and sore. And terrified. She struggled to free her hands, which they had tied behind her back with a piece of rough rope. Rather than freeing herself, she only managed to rub her wrists raw.

*Please, God, help me. Please let me get free of these men. Let me go back to Jackson so I can tell him how much I care about him.*

Her thoughts surprised her. Had she really developed such deep feelings for Jackson so quickly? Was it possible that she loved him?

Terror quickly turned to despair as the sun rose higher in the sky and no one from the ranch arrived to rescue her. Her lips cracked from being dry, her head ached, and she could feel the sun burning her skin. She wondered whether Jackson even knew what had happened to her. And she wondered if Shorty was alright, if they had managed to stop his bleeding and patch his wound.

As she had lain across the back of the horse on her belly,

each step bruising her ribs and forcing the air from her lungs, she'd overheard the outlaws planning and didn't like what she'd heard one bit. They were planning to ransom her to Jackson for a lot of money. Samuel had some wild notion that Jackson owed him for having gotten in the way when she arrived to marry him. Even though he never had any intention of marrying anyone, but only stealing from her.

But Jackson would have no reason to pay a ransom for her safe return. She was merely his cook and housekeeper, nothing more. Unless ...? Could she even dream that she meant more to him than he let on?

"She's awake," Buster called out to Samuel.

"Good. Now look here, missy. You came out here to marry me! What do you mean going and living with Trimble. I suppose you gave him the money you promised to give me?"

Catherine stared at the man in stunned silence at his outrageous claims. Finally, she said, "You lied to me. You lied about who you were and you never intended to marry anyone. You were only going to rob me!"

Samuel was shoved out of the way by Buster who squatted down and got right in her face.

"We got ourselves a lively one, Sam. Let's say we have a little fun. Pretend she's our new bride and it's the wedding night." Buster cackled, showing a mouth full of rotten teeth as he moved closer to Catherine and attempted to kiss her neck.

She recoiled and pulled her head back as far as possible, but it thudded on the back of the tree where they had placed her on the ground, and she saw stars.

Buster clasped his hands around her throat, forcing her

to open her eyes in panic. Samuel immediately pulled him away from her, "I told you not to hurt her! Trimble's gonna be mad enough when he pays the ransom. I don't want to spend the rest of my life running from him to keep it."

"What are you so afraid of? He hasn't fought for years. He's rusty and that will make him both slow and inaccurate."

As Buster finished the last syllable of his word, a bullet flew past his head, nicking the top of his ear and causing him to fall, belly-down on the ground. "What the .... !"

"Get the woman!" Samuel shouted.

"Leave the woman alone!" came back an instant reply from the depths of the trees. "Don't move!"

Catherine searched frantically for the location of the voice. It wasn't Jackson's she heard, and she only hoped the men out there with their guns drawn were friends and not more foes she needed to worry about.

"Texas Rangers! Thrown down your weapons and get down on the ground. Now!"

Buster was trying to crawl behind a copse of sage brush when another bullet rang out, this one hitting him in the hand he had outstretched on the ground.

"Owiee!"

Catherine tried to scoot back, wanting to get as far away from the bullets that seemed to be coming closer to her with every movement Buster made. Out of the corner of her eye, she saw Samuel Cardwell scurry into the brush and start to run.

"He's getting away!" she shouted to the uniformed Texas Ranger who had Buster pinned to the ground, knee in his back as he lay writhing on his belly.

"He won't get far, ma'am. We've got the place surround-ed." The Ranger finished handcuffing Buster and stood up.

He lifted Catherine gently to her feet. "I'm Wilson Sawyer with the Texas Rangers. Turn around and let me cut that rope off your wrists. Hold still now, so I don't cut you in the process."

Catherine stood still while the Ranger cut the rope that bound her wrists. When it snapped, she brought her arms around in front of her and gently massaged the raw skin.

"WHAT DO YOU MEAN, he got away!" Ranger Sawyer and Jackson shouted the words simultaneously as the two younger rangers tried to explain how they lost Samuel Cardwell's trail.

The Ranger had travelled from the town, where he had taken Catherine to be examined by a doctor, to Jackson's ranch to check to see whether Cardwell had appeared there. While he and Jackson were speaking, the two rangers who had gone in pursuit of Cardwell arrived, exhausted and empty-handed.

"He had to have crossed the river," the shorter of the rangers said. "It was a big area and we were tracking him through the forest for a couple of miles. Suddenly lost all signs of him."

The tall, slender man elaborated. "The snapped twigs indicated he had taken the upwards path at the fork. But when we got to the top of the hill, there was no sign of him and we could hear the river flowing below us. Figured we went the wrong way."

"When will the posse be formed?" Jackson asked. "Cardwell won't rest until he gets his revenge."

Ranger Sawyer hesitated, digging his toe into the ground as he took off his hat and scratched his head.

"Well, Mr. Trimble, I'm not so sure this warrants a posse," he said. "We're on the tail of some worse outlaws right now and I don't have any men I can give up."

"Worse? Cardwell assaulted a young woman and shot my foreman."

The Ranger looked straight at Jackson. "As much as I sympathize, the band of outlaws we're chasing robbed two banks and killed four people, one of them a lawman. The delay we took today to save Miss Lamott and capture one of these two scoundrels has put us further behind in our pursuit." He paused. "I'm sorry, Mr. Trimble."

The three rangers left Jackson standing on the porch, mounted their horses and rode away. Jackson realized he would have to take matters into his own hands if he expected to keep Cardwell away from Catherine. The wretched outlaw somehow had it in his head that Jackson stood in the way of his chance to separate Catherine from some non-existent fortune.

He wanted to check on Shorty's condition first, but then Jackson would head into town where Catherine was being looked after by George and Miriam. He had a decision to make.

CATHERINE WAS RESTING in the small bedroom that she'd used when she first arrived in Texarkana and stayed with George and Miriam while contemplating her future. It felt strangely comfortable, like a warm cocoon of a place, much like her childhood home.

After she had been rescued by the Ranger, they had crossed paths with Jackson and his men on the search for her and Samuel Cardwell. The Ranger explained what had happened in the woods and assured Jackson that his men would have Cardwell in handcuffs before sunset. Buster, who was at that moment tied and flung across his horse, much like Catherine had been earlier in the day, would be taken to the jail.

The Ranger had insisted that he would escort Catherine to town so she could be examined by a doctor and then taken to the Smythson's, where Miriam would look after her, tend to her bruises and see that she got proper nourishment. They all felt it would be safer for her as well, with Cardwell still at large.

Ranger Sawyer had convinced Jackson to return to his ranch in case Cardwell took the opportunity to ambush it, thinking that all the men would be out hunting for him. It was not unknown for outlaws to burn down the property of those they wanted to harm and Samuel Cardwell was certainly the type that would not hesitate such an action.

Doc Jackson had cleaned and bandaged Catherine's bruises, none of which were serious. She was sore and dehydrated, but the Doc thought she was well enough to recuperate at the Smythson's.

"Let me help you sit up, dear," said Miriam. She had slipped into the room quietly with a bowl of broth on a tray and fresh pitcher of water. She slipped her arms under Catherine's and helped the younger woman sit up, fluffing her pillows and then gently lowering her back.

Miriam sat on the edge of the bed and placed the tray on Catherine's lap, handed her the spoon and watched with concern as Catherine took a few tentative sips of the warm liquid.

As she was finishing the soup, George tapped softly on the bedroom door and stuck his head around the corner.

"How's our patient doing?" he asked.

"Much better, thanks to you both," said Catherine.

Miriam nodded her head in agreement, clearly happy to see the color returning to Catherine's cheeks.

"Up for a visitor?" George asked.

Before she had time to respond, George opened the door wider and the women saw Jackson standing behind him, hat in his hands.

Catherine pulled the dressing gown that Miriam had loaned her tighter around her neck and nodded. A wave of relief and joy swelled in her chest when she saw Jackson.

He slipped around George and entered the small bedroom, taking the rickety wooden chair from the corner and placing it beside the bed. Miriam hesitated, not wanting to leave them alone, but George reached out for her hand and tugged his wife gently away. When she looked questioningly at Catherine, the younger woman nodded that she would be fine.

After the door closed softly behind the Smythsons and their footsteps could be heard descending the staircase, Jackson sat stiffly on the modest chair.

"How are you feeling?" he asked.

"I'm fine, thank you," Catherine replied. "I should be able to resume my duties at the ranch tomorrow. Miriam insists that I should spend tonight here."

Jackson cleared his throat.

"Miss Lamott," he began. "Catherine. I've checked the schedule, and the next train returning to St. Louis is the day after tomorrow. I've purchased your ticket, and I've also placed your wages in this purse." He handed her a blue satin bag with drawstring, but she did not reach for it. "I think you'll find the amount generous enough to help you start a new life."

Catherine stared at Jackson. She felt numb and no

words would come to her lips. "Why .... ?" Her voice quivered and she could not halt the tear that escaped her eye and ran down her check.

Jackson stood up, unable to look her in the eye. "I think it's best." He slipped out of the room and down the stairs.

## 13

When the two rangers had returned empty-handed, Jackson was devastated that he had missed the opportunity to capture Cardwell. He should not have listened to Ranger Sawyer and returned to guard his ranch, but hunted down Samuel Cardwell until he had captured the dirty thug and made sure that he was never in a position to harm another innocent person.

After searching his soul, Jackson decided that he could no longer put Catherine at risk. He was fond of her while at the same time disquieted by the depth of his feelings. But with Cardwell loose, how could he expect her to stay at his ranch just to see where their feelings might lead? They would always expect the next strike and she would never feel completely safe.

She would be better off back in St. Louis, a more civilized place than Texarkana. Perhaps if Cardwell was caught and convicted, Jackson could write to her and ask her to return someday.

He shook that thought from his head. Asking the woman he loved to travel across dangerous territory to become his wife is what broke him two years earlier. He would not contemplate that thought again.

It was then that he had decided his only option was to purchase her train ticket and send her on her way home with enough of a nest egg to start a new life. He owed her that much, after having interfered in her life to begin with.

CATHERINE WAS inconsolable after Jackson left. There was nothing George or Miriam could say to stop her tears and she could be heard crying herself to sleep. Miriam had tried to convince Catherine that she could stay with them while she continued to respond to ads to become a mail order bride, but Catherine declined. She had sensed they were struggling at the mercantile and she did not want to be a burden to them.

By morning, Catherine was spent. She had no tears left when she descended the stairs from her room to the kitchen where she joined the Smythsons for breakfast. Miriam ached for the girl, whose cheeks were pale, eyes red and rimmed with dark circles.

Jackson had asked the Smythsons if they would be so kind as to bring Catherine out to the ranch to collect her personal things. He would be out in the fields all day herding cattle so they would not have to endure a painful goodbye.

The three of them travelled along the rutted dirt path in silence, two horses pulling George's wagon and its passengers. As they drove, Catherine soaked in the fresh air and sunlight, lifting her face to its warmth. There was both beauty and danger in the vastness of the changing terrain and she knew she would be forever changed by having spent time in this place.

As George set the hand brake on the wagon in front of the house, Catherine twisted in her seat, straining her neck in hope of catching a glimpse of Jackson in the fields. Surely he was not going to let her leave without saying goodbye.

"They're miles away, my dear," George said, reading Catherine's mind. "Pushing a herd to the north end where they just finished building that new corral."

George and Miriam each took one of her arms and led her up the stairs into the house.

Once she had packed her scanty belongings, she returned to the living room where her guardians waited. Miriam had offered to help her pack, but Catherine preferred solitude in the room she had called home for only a short time, but where she'd felt a sense of security despite the encounters with Cardwell.

In the living room, she set down her satchel and, as if in a daze, moved to the piano. She dreamily ran her fingers over the keys and, completely forgetting that the Smythsons were in the room with her, she started to play.

As she struck the keys with emotion, the piece reaching its crescendo, Catherine did not notice that Shorty had joined them, limping into the room on crutches. When the reverberation subsided and the house had become quiet once more, the foreman broke the silence.

"No wonder he's been so despondent lately."

"I'm sorry, I did not realize anyone was in the house." Catherine stood up from the piano and moved to pick up her satchel. "How are you recovering, Shorty?" she asked.

"I'm mending fine, Miss Catherine." He made his way to an oversize chair and sat down heavily, having worn himself out with the effort.

"What was that you said?" Catherine recalled Shorty's words when she first stopped playing. "Who is despondent?"

"Jackson," Shorty responded. "He knows you play?"

"Yes, the day I arrived. I did not know he was in the house and lost myself in the music. He was behind me when I finished."

"Ah."

"What is it Shorty?" Catherine asked. "Who did this piano belong to?"

"I think that's something you should hear from Jackson," he said. Shorty pulled himself up on his crutches and limped towards the door. "You take good care of yourself, Miss Catherine."

"And you." Catherine turned back to George and Miriam who had been silently watching the exchange. "I'm ready."

DINNER at the ranch was solemn. The men were physically exhausted from the long ride out to the north fields and back. Jackson did not normally push them so hard on a single day. They also missed Catherine, having enjoyed her cooking and the company of a woman at their mid-day meal.

Today's meal was a mediocre stew that Shorty had thrown together in a pinch. He was staying at Jackson's house while his injury mended and wanted to make himself useful. He tossed onions, carrots and potatoes into a large pot, along with a rump of beef, and tried to replicate one of the dishes that Catherine made, but all of them picked at the tough meat and undercooked vegetables.

Jackson told the ranchers to go home rather than

resume working until sundown. They had done enough for one day and Jackson himself did not have the energy to continue. Instead, he helped clear the table and took the dishes to Shorty who had propped himself against the sink, leaning on his crutches, to wash the plates, cutlery and pot.

"Ain't no reason to send her away." Shorty finally broke the silence.

Jackson looked up, surprised that his foreman would opine on a personal matter.

As he carried the last of the dirty plates to the sink, he replied, "Got every reason."

"It's not the same as Isabel," Shorty prodded. "Miss Catherine accepts who you are and isn't asking you to change your life for her. She was happy here. A man can tell."

Jackson stared at Shorty with steely eyes, grabbed a shot glass and a bottle of whiskey from the cupboard, and stormed out of the kitchen onto the porch, letting the door slam behind him.

"Stubborn fool." Shorty scraped the last of the burned meat from the bottom of the pot.

## 14

T he morning dawned gray and overcast, with the whisper of a light mist in the air. George, Miriam and Catherine were subdued as they ate breakfast in the Smythson's kitchen.

Miriam had packed several sandwiches for Catherine to take on her train journey, some apples, and seltzer water. She also wrapped a big fat pickle, a chunk of sharp cheese and half a loaf of bread. As she was wrapping a sweet pastry made with cinnamon, Catherine protested.

"I shall never finish all of it, Miriam. Do keep something here for you and George."

"It's a long journey, my dear, and I've heard that the food available on the trains is downright inedible."

Jackson had purchased a first class ticket in a sleeper car for Catherine, so her journey home to St. Louis would be far more comfortable than the rough, cramped passage to Texarkana a month earlier. It felt like a lifetime ago, and Catherine recalled her excitement and anticipation on that trip. While she would be more physically comfortable this time, her heart was heavy and she did not look forward to the long trip ahead.

The bell rang on the door to the mercantile which allowed Miriam to give Catherine a swift hug and wish for safe travels before dashing into the front of the store to take care of the arriving customer. Both women were grateful to escape the outpouring of tears that was sure to come if they lingered over their goodbye.

George pulled the collar up around his neck, placed his hat on his head, and picked up Catherine's satchel. He handed her a colorful umbrella from the mercantile.

"Something to remember us by," he said, his voice catching in his throat.

"I will never forget either one of you," Catherine said, blinking back tears. She opened the red and white striped umbrella and held it over the two of them as best she could.

They walked to the station in silence and only after arriving on the platform did George speak again.

"I'm sorry it didn't work out. Not sure I even understand why it didn't."

Catherine sighed. "I'm not sure I totally understand either, George. I thought he cared about me." It was almost too much to bear, this recall of what might have gone wrong.

"If there's one thing I know, it's people," George said. "And sure as I'm standing here, that man cared a great deal for you. He's haunted by something and I'll be darned if I know what it is. But he's making a terrible mistake."

The stationmaster appeared on the platform and approached George and Catherine.

"You folks waitin' for the trans-con headed to St. Louis?"

"That's right," George replied.

"Runnin' a bit late. Be 'bout an hour." The stationmaster

hurried along and descended the platform, not wanting to entertain any questions about the matter.

The rain had become more steady and George was half-soaked, having insisted that Catherine use the umbrella to keep herself dry rather than try to shield the two of them. She would be wearing the clothes she had on for a long time and it was best they didn't start out wet.

"You go ahead home, George," she said. "I'll be fine. You're soaked to the skin and this is your busy morning at the mercantile. Miriam could use your help."

"Alright, darlin', if you're sure." He exhaled in relief as he dug into his pocket. When he pulled his hand out, he pressed it into her hand.

Catherine felt the gold coin and knew it was a financial strain for him to give her money. She could not accept this, in addition to everything else these kind, dear people had done for her. She pushed back, pressing the gold coin into George's palm and closing his fist around it.

"No, I cannot take this," she said. "Jackson gave me a very generous purse. I shall have more than enough to start over when I get back to St. Louis."

She sensed George's hesitation.

"Miriam and I discussed this, and we agreed." He made a feeble attempt to push back, but their hardship was real and he was grateful that Catherine refused the gesture. "But if you're absolutely sure."

Catherine retrieved the blue satin purse from the inside pocket of her skirt where she had tied the drawstring to her garments for safety. She opened the purse slightly so George could see inside. "You see, I'll be just fine."

They hugged their good-byes, both having a difficult time letting go of the tight bear hug. George wished her well and Catherine told him to take good care of Miriam, and she promised to write as soon as she arrived in St. Louis and let them know she was well.

Catherine watched George lumber down the stairs of the train platform and walk back to the mercantile, shoulders slumped. She stood staring at the last spot she could see him for several minutes after he had turned the corner and was out of view.

She was so deep in her thoughts, with the rain falling harder and thunder rumbling in the distance, that she did not hear the footsteps behind her.

"Ok, little lady, we're going to end our relationship here once and for all."

Catherine spun around as the raspy voice of Samuel Cardwell assaulted her ears. He was merely feet away from her and her eyes darted along the platform. They were alone.

"He, he, he," he cackled. "Didn't see me over behind that post, did ya."

Catherine froze. She had no weapon and with the rain and thunder, was certain her scream would not be heard.

"You'll learn to be more careful from now on," Cardwell taunted. "I ain't gonna hurt ya. I just want that purse." He pointed to her waist where she had re-fastened the satin purse Jackson had given her after showing it to George.

How could she have been so stupid?

"Step back, Cardwell."

A voice boomed over the thunder and Catherine did not need to look to recognize it.

"Stay outta this, Trimble!" Cardwell yelled. "She has nothin' to do with you any more."

"Catherine, move back slowly." Jackson's voice was composed and even.

"I'm warnin' you!" Cardwell shouted while simultaneously reaching his hand to his hip.

CRACK!

Before Samuel Cardwell's hand was halfway to his holster, Jackson had drawn and fired, hitting Cardwell directly in the center of the chest.

He fell to ground on the platform and Jackson approached him cautiously, ensuring he was unable to draw his gun, before turning to Catherine to see that she was alright.

The stationmaster ran up the stairs, followed by Jeb from the feed store. The next several minutes were chaos for Catherine while it was determined that Cardwell was indeed dead. She had never seen a man killed before and hoped to never witness such a scene again. But she could not say she was sorry that Jackson had done what he had.

GEORGE, Miriam, Jackson and Catherine all sat around the Smythson's dining table sipping tea and collecting their thoughts from the events of the day.

First and foremost, Catherine wanted to know how Jackson came to be at the train station. Had he finally realized that they needed to say a proper goodbye to one another? That without it, neither of them would have closure?

Just after George and Catherine had left for the station that morning, Jackson arrived at the mercantile to collect his weekly supplies. What he had not expected was a fearless berating from Miriam that was akin to a lioness protecting her cub. How could Jackson have treated Catherine so? Did he not realize that she loved him? Did he not care for her at all?

Jackson responded defensively. No, he said, he did not know she loved him. How should he have known this? And yes, he did care for her. Of course, he did, which is why he knew he had to let her go. It was for her own good, and her safety. He did not want blood on his hands again. Did not want to be responsible for the death of another woman he loved.

Jackson had nothing to lose by explaining to Miriam the reason for his behavior. The only other person in Texarkana who knew Jackson's background from his lawman days was Shorty, and he was intensely loyal. Jackson knew that the townspeople of Texarkana were curious about his past and now was the time to tell someone.

And so he told Miriam about Isabel, the love of his life, his fiancé.

Jackson was a Texas Ranger living and working in Odessa, Texas. He was a legendary lawman, tough but fair, a fast draw who knew when to use force and when to exercise constraint. Isabel was never comfortable with his choice of profession, but he assured her that his line of work was no more dangerous that that of any other occupation in the west.

Isabel was a refined lady and was having difficulty settling in Odessa. She had grown up with her parents in Dallas, her mother's home town, in a fine estate where she wore elegant gowns and learned to play the piano. When her mother died tragically, her grandparents never forgave Isabel's father whom they thought was to blame. He was forced to leave Dallas and return to his own home town of Odessa, a small rugged town with few women and many outlaws, taking his daughter with him. Before long, Isabel met Jackson and fell in love with the kind, dignified ranger.

One night, he had been leading a group of fellow rangers to find and capture a band of violent outlaws who had been terrorizing west Texas for nearly a year. The rangers had finally received a reliable tip that three of the gang were hiding out in a saloon. Jackson wanted to surround the bar and wait for the men to depart before ambushing them. But a blunder by one of the rangers resulted in them rushing the place unprepared, with a gunfight ensuing.

When his fellow rangers delivered Jackson home with a bullet in his leg, Isabel had had enough. She told him she would not stand by and watch him die, nor sit at home day and night wondering where he was and what danger he was facing. A few days later, she took a train back to Dallas to live with a spinster aunt.

Within a month, Jackson had hung up his badge and moved east. He purchased the ranch in Texarkana and wrote to Isabel, begging her to come back to him. To entice her, he told her he had purchased a piano for her and described the ranch home and beautiful landscape. It had been a promise that Jackson had made to her when they became engaged, that he would find a way for her to have her beloved piano again.

Isabel quickly accepted Jackson's renewed proposal and penned him a letter that she was on her way in the stage-coach from Dallas, too impatient to wait for the train that had a very irregular schedule at the time. While on her way to become his wife, the stagecoach she was traveling in was attacked by bandits and Isabel was killed.

When Jackson finished his story, Miriam sat quietly for a moment in deference to his anguish as he relived the tragedy all over again just by sharing it. But she also wanted to convince him that his past experience, however painful, should not be used as an excuse to reject a new chance at love now.

"Deep in your heart, you must know it is not logical to push Catherine away because of what happened in the past." Miriam wanted to shake Jackson who was now sitting at the counter of the mercantile with his head bowed, all energy depleted from the retelling of the loss of his Isabel.

"It is too late now in any case." He raised his wrist and looked at his watch. "The train left the station eight minutes ago."

As if on cue, George entered the mercantile. He took off his soaked overcoat and hat, stepped back onto the porch and shook them out before re-entering the shop and hanging both on a hook.

"Has she left?" Miriam asked. "Did you see her safely onto the train?"

George shook his head. "Train's delayed about an hour. She didn't want me to wait with her."

Could this be fate? A sign from God? Jackson looked at Miriam and then back at George.

"Don't just sit there, man. Run!" Miriam whooped as she gave Jackson a shove and practically pushed him out the door.

## 15

"Miss Catherine, play us a song!"

"With pleasure, Shorty." Catherine stood up from the dinner table and started to clear the dishes. "But wouldn't you like dessert first? Miriam made apple pie."

Jackson stood up as well and started gathering the plates at his end of the table. "You are awfully demanding of my wife there, Shorty." He laughed good-naturedly. "First she cooks Sunday dinner for you and you also expect her to clean up *and* entertain?"

Shorty followed the lead of his hosts and carried his plate to the sink. "I'll do the clean up. I got used to it during my recuperation. I swear, Jackson, the only reason you invited me to stay after I was shot was to do the cleaning after you sent this little lady away."

It had been a week since the episode at the train platform. After the dust had settled and Catherine had learned that Jackson's ambivalence about their relationship had come from his guilt over Isabel's death, she was able to reconcile his actions and understand that he was not rejecting her. He was afraid that the same fate would befall her as had Isabel.

Catherine had stayed with George and Miriam that night but Jackson had promised to return the following morning so they could talk about their future. She hoped he would agree to have her return as his cook and housekeeper, to give them both time to get to know one another better. To see where their feelings led.

Catherine had come to realize that rushing into marriage with someone she barely knew, as she was about to do when she came west as a mail order bride to a complete stranger, was a bit imprudent. And while she believed she was falling in love with Jackson, she understood that he needed time after everything he had been through.

As a result, no one was more surprised than Catherine when Jackson turned up the following morning in a suit and tie, carrying a bouquet of wildflowers, with Shorty beside him in the wagon.

"What are you doing coming all the way to town, Shorty." Catherine had stepped onto the porch of the mercantile when she heard Jackson's wagon pull up. She knew that Shorty was not fond of leaving the ranch. And considering he was still limping around on crutches, it was even more unusual.

"Boss insisted," Shorty said. "And you know how demanding he can be when he wants something." He laughed as George helped him down from the wagon, and Jackson handed his crutches to him.

Catherine shielded her eyes against the sun as she gazed up at Jackson. He was handsome, and he looked especially dashing this morning with a little smirk on his lips and eyes that seemed to smile.

"I had to bring someone along as a best man." Jackson jumped down from the wagon directly in front of Catherine, bowed to her and held out the bouquet of flowers. "That is, if you'll marry me.'

Miriam squealed with glee and George grabbed Jackson by the shoulders, pulled him in for a hug and patted him on the back.

"I hoped you would both be witnesses," Jackson said to the Smythsons. "Preacher said he'd do it today. Although I still have not had an answer from my intended."

Four sets of eyes turned towards Catherine who was still speechless by this public display and Jackson's proposal.

"I don't know what to say," she said. "It's all so sudden. I thought you wanted us to have more time to get to know each other."

"I don't stand much on ceremony, Catherine. And I've made a lot of mistakes. In the past, and recently." Jackson took her hand. "But I do love you, and I think you love me. And I think it would be awfully difficult to have you under my roof as my cook and housekeeper and not my wife. That would just be a scandal waiting to happen and I don't think George and Miriam would approve."

Miriam put her hands on her hips, but was laughing. "You've got that right, mister."

"What do you say?" Jackson clasped both Catherine's hands in his and looked her directly in the eyes. "Will you marry me?"

"Yes, oh yes, of course," Catherine laughed and cried at the same time as she threw her arms around Jackson's neck and hugged him with all her might.

He lifted her in the air, let out a holler, and shouted, "Then let's all get to the preacher."

As he lowered Catherine to the ground, he tightened his arms around her waist and looked deep into her eyes.

"I love you, my darling," he said.

"And I love you."

Catherine lifted her head and smiled as her fiancé kissed her lips.

"I'll never let you go."

### THE END

# ABOUT THE AUTHOR

Cassie Malone lives in Grand Junction, Colorado with her husband and two teenage children. When she isn't shuttling her son to basketball or her daughter to dance, she writes western historical romance with inspiration from views of the Colorado National Monument from her home office window.